Test Stress

by Jamie Hector and Alaine Roberson

Illustrated by Rachel Moss

ISBN: 978-1-338-83220-4

Editors: Maria L. Chang, Pari Deshpande Cohen, and Lynne M. Wilson
Art Director: Tannaz Fassihi; Designer: Cynthia Ng

1 2 3 4 5 6 7 8 9 10 68 30 29 28 27 26 25 24 23

Printed in Jiaxing, China. First printing, January 2023.

SCHOLASTIC

Chloé is very sad. She had taken a spelling test. She got more words wrong than she got right.

Chloé is worried that she is not as smart as her friends.

Chloé asks, “Ms. Baker, why did I fail the test?”
“Sometimes we fail, Chloé,” answers her teacher. “But it’s okay. Study and you will do better next time.”

"But I did study!" says Chloé.

"It's just one test, Chloé," says Ms. Baker. "Try not to worry so much."

When Dad picks up Chloé from school, she looks very sad.

Dad asks, "What's wrong, Chloé? Why do you look sad?"

"I failed my spelling test," says Chloé. She begins to cry.

“I don’t think I am smart enough. All my friends got higher scores than I did,” cries Chloé.

“You are smart, Chloé. Don’t cry,” says Dad. “Did you study for your test?”

“Yes, I studied,” says Chloé, still crying. “But when I was taking the test, I got so scared that I forgot how to spell.”

“Why were you scared?” asks Dad.

“I didn’t want to fail,” cries Chloé.

“Well, that explains what happened,” says Dad. “You were very worried, and that caused stress. Some people don’t work well when they feel stressed.”

"Chloé, take a big, deep breath in. Then let it out very slowly as you count to 10," says Dad.

Chloé takes a really deep breath and counts to 10 on her fingers as she lets out the air.

"Now say, 'I can do this,'" says Dad.
"I can do this," says Chloé softly.
"Do it again," says Dad.

Chloé takes a deep breath in and lets it out slowly, counting to 10.

"I can do it!" she says more firmly.

"One more time," says Dad.

Chloé takes one more deep breath.

"I got this!" she exclaims.

“Do you feel better?” asks Dad.
“Yes, I do!” smiles Chloé. “Thanks, Dad!”

The following week, Chloé has another spelling test.

"I got this!" Chloé says softly. She takes a deep breath and picks up her pencil.

Chloé's New Hairdo

by Jamie Hector and Alaine Roberson

Illustrated by Rachel Moss

ISBN: 978-1-338-83219-8

Editors: Maria L. Chang, Pari Deshpande Cohen, and Lynne M. Wilson
Art Director: Tannaz Fassihi; Designer: Cynthia Ng

1 2 3 4 5 6 7 8 9 10 68 30 29 28 27 26 25 24 23

Printed in Jiaxing, China. First printing, January 2023.

SCHOLASTIC

Every morning, Chloé's mom brushes her hair just so.

But when she picks Chloé up from school, Chloé's hair never looks the same.

One day, Chloé's mom asks, "What happened to your hair?"

“I don’t know,” Chloé replies. “My hair is just not. . .”

"Not what?" asks Mom.

"My hair is not long, it's not short, it's not straight, it's not wavy. It's just not right!"

"I think your hair is just right. Maybe what you need is a new hairdo," says Mom. "Let's go to the hair salon."

"Chloé says her hair is not right," Mom tells her hair stylist, Malika.

"Lots of girls think that, Chloé," says Malika. "But your hair is just right for you!"

"It is?" asks Chloé. "Why is my hair just right for me?"

"Because it is perfectly made for you! No one else has your hair," she says. "Your hair tells the world who you are and where you're from."

“It does?” asks Chloé. “But why won’t my hair stay straight like Amber’s or wavy like Maria’s?”

“Because Amber’s family has straight hair, and Maria’s family has wavy hair,” says Mom.

“Your hair isn’t like theirs,” says Malika. “When you try to do your hair like theirs, it doesn’t stay. We just need to find the style that’s right for you.”

Malika begins to comb Chloé's hair.

"Your hair is soft and fluffy, but it's also nice and strong. Let's see what we can do."

Chloé looks through the pages of Malika's book.

She sees long blond hairstyles, curly red hairstyles, and straight black hairstyles.

She sees drop curl styles and short styles.
She sees big afros and twist-and-lock styles.

Finally, Chloé sees the style that is just right for her!

“This is it!” exclaims Chloé. “This is the style for me!”

“I like it!” says Malika.

“It’s perfect!” agrees Mom.

Malika gets to work washing and drying Chloé's hair. Then she parts Chloé's hair and puts hair oil in the parts. Malika begins to braid each section.

Soon, Malika is done. She hands Chloé a mirror and lets her take a look.

"What do you think, Chloé?"

"I love it!" smiles Chloé. "This style is just right for me! My hair is just right for me!"

Chloé to the Rescue!

by Jamie Hector and Alaine Roberson

Illustrated by Rachel Moss

ISBN: 978-1-338-83222-8

Editors: Maria L. Chang, Pari Deshpande Cohen, and Lynne M. Wilson
Art Director: Tannaz Fassihi; Designer: Cynthia Ng

1 2 3 4 5 6 7 8 9 10 68 30 29 28 27 26 25 24 23

Printed in Jiaxing, China. First printing, January 2023.

SCHOLASTIC

Chloé's mom and dad are busy painting the living room.

“Mom!” Sajés calls from the top of the staircase.

Mom says, “Chloé, go check on Sajés, please.”

“Why?” asks Chloé.

“Because your dad and I are busy, and you are his big sister. We need you to help watch him,” Mom replies.

Chloé runs upstairs. Sajés does not look happy.

"I'm stuck," he says. Sajés points to his foot stuck between the wooden bars by the stairs.

Chloé looks at his foot.

"Oh, my goodness," says Chloé.

“I want Mommy!” cries Sajés.

“Mom and Dad are busy. I’m your big sister. I’ll help!” Chloé runs downstairs.

“Dad, what would you do if your foot were stuck between wooden bars?” she asks.

“I would take my shoe and sock off,” Dad says.

“That should do it!” exclaims Chloé.

She runs back upstairs.

“I’m going to take your shoe and sock off. Then your foot will slide out,” says Chloé.

Chloé pulls off his sneaker and sock. But Sajés is still stuck.

“Awwww, man,” Sajés says.

“Awwww, man,” echoes Chloé. “Don’t worry, I will save you!”

“I want Mommy,” whines Sajés.

Chloé runs downstairs to her grandmother in the kitchen cooking dinner.

"Grandma, what would you do if your foot were stuck between wooden bars?"

"I would rub my foot with oil and then slide my foot right out!" says Grandma.

"Thank you!" says Chloé.

Chloé runs back up to Sajés. She rubs baby oil on his foot.

"Okay, Sajés. Slide your foot out!" orders Chloé.

Sajés pulls and pulls. But his foot does not come out.

"Awww, man!" says Sajés.

"Awww, man!" repeats Chloé.

Sajés looks at Chloé and says, "Try, try again!"

Chloé runs back downstairs.

"Mom! What would you do if your foot were stuck between two wooden bars?"

"Well, how did I get stuck in the first place?" Mom asks.

"Why does that matter?" asks Chloé.

"If you know how you got stuck, then you might know how to get unstuck," answers Mom.

"Okay, got it!" Chloé exclaims.

Chloé runs back upstairs.

"Sajés, how did you get stuck?" she asks.

Sajés points to the middle of the wooden bars. The middle is narrower than the bottom.

"Ooooooh," says Chloé, thinking.

Chloé lifts Sajés's foot to the middle of the bar. It slides right out!

"Thank you, Chloé!" exclaims Sajés happily.

“I saved him! I’m a good big sister!” Chloé smiles to herself.

Sajés's Birthday Feast

by Jamie Hector and Alaine Roberson

Illustrated by Rachel Moss

ISBN: 978-1-338-83221-1

Editors: Maria L. Chang, Pari Deshpande Cohen, and Lynne M. Wilson
Art Director: Tannaz Fassihi; Designer: Cynthia Ng

1 2 3 4 5 6 7 8 9 10 68 30 29 28 27 26 25 24 23

Printed in Jiaxing, China. First printing, January 2023.

SCHOLASTIC

Chloé sits with her dad on the sofa. Today is her little brother Sajés's birthday. Everyone will be coming over to celebrate.

Grandma Hector is in the kitchen cooking black rice. She calls out, “Chloé, *vin gade*!”

"What did she say?" whispers Chloé.

"Chloé, come look!" says Dad.

"Why does Grandma Hector speak Creole?" Chloé asks.

"Because she was born in Haiti," says Dad.

“She sounds funny!” Chloé laughs.
“It’s not nice to laugh,” says Dad.

The doorbell rings. Chloé runs to the door. It's Grandma Prescod!

"Chloé girl, ya gettin' so tall," she says with a Bajan accent.

"Why do you talk so funny, Grandma? You sound like you are singing a song," Chloé giggles.

“I’m from Barbados,” she says. “We don’t sound funny. *You* would sound funny in Barbados.”

Grandma Prescod goes to the kitchen to help Grandma Hector.

“Why don’t you and Mommy talk like Grandma Hector and Grandma Prescod?” Chloé asks her dad.

“Because we were born here in the United States. But your grandmothers were not,” explains Dad. “They have accents from their homelands.”

“What’s a homeland?” asks Chloé.

“It’s the country you are born in,” Dad answers. “Your language, family traditions, music, and the way you dress all come from your homeland. Laughing at people because of where they are from is hurtful.”

“Sajés, your guests are here!” says Mom. “Let’s open the door for them!”

José walks in with his mother, Ms. Maria.

"*Feliz cumpleaños,* Sajés," greets José.

"He said, 'Happy Birthday,'" says Dad.

"Is that how you speak in your homeland, José?" asks Chloé.

"Yes. We are from Puerto Rico, and we speak Spanish," says José. "We brought mofongo and a birthday gift!"

Aadir and his mother Binita come next.

"*Namaste,*" say Aadir and Binita.

"Is that what they say in your homeland?" asks Chloé.

"Yes, we are from India," Binita answers. "We brought naan and butter chicken."

"My favorite!" says Aadir.

Ella runs in and gives Sajés a birthday gift.

“Thank you!” says Sajés.

“We brought macaroni and cheese,” Mr. Taylor announces.

“How come you don’t have an accent, Mr.Taylor?” Chloé asks.

“I have an accent,” says Mr. Taylor. “I have an American accent, like you!”

“Everything smells so good!” Mom exclaims.

“I love that we have food from all over the world!” Sajés beams.

“We’re so lucky to have friends from so many different homelands,” says Chloé.

Dad smiles at her proudly.

Why Is Butter Sad?

by Jamie Hector and Alaine Roberson
Illustrated by Rachel Moss

ISBN: 978-1-338-83223-5

Editors: Maria L. Chang, Pari Deshpande Cohen, and Lynne M. Wilson
Art Director: Tannaz Fassihi; Designer: Cynthia Ng

1 2 3 4 5 6 7 8 9 10 68 30 29 28 27 26 25 24 23

Printed in Jiaxing, China. First printing, January 2023.

SCHOLASTIC

Chloé has a cat named Butter. Butter likes to play.

One day, Sajés asks Chloé, "Can I feed Butter?"

"Okay," says Chloé. "But don't feed her too much."

"Okay," replies Sajés. "Come, Butter, come eat!"

Sajés runs off, and Butter follows him.

Later that day, Butter does not want to play.
“Butter won’t play with me, Chloé,” pouts Sajés.

Chloé rubs Butter's fur, but Butter does not purr.

"Why do you look so sad?" Chloé asks Butter.

"Dad, why is Butter sad?" Chloé asks her father.

Dad comes in to look at Butter. Butter rubs on Chloé's legs.

“Why is Butter rubbing on my legs?” asks Chloé.

“I don’t know,” answers Dad. “She’s your cat. Maybe she is trying to tell you something.”

“But cats can’t talk, can they?” asks Chloé.

“Meow,” says Butter.

“Should we take Butter to our doctor?” Chloé asks her dad.

"No, our doctor does not see cats," explains Dad. "Butter needs an animal doctor."

"Animals have doctors?" asks Chloé.

"Yes, they are called veterinarians," replies Dad. "We call them vets for short."

"Can we take Butter to a vet?" asks Chloé.

"Maybe," says Dad. "First, see if you can figure out what's wrong with her."

Chloé looks at Butter's head. It looks fine.

She looks at Butter's eyes, nose, and mouth. Butter lies down.

"Meow," says Butter.

Chloé rubs Butter's back. It feels fine. She checks her legs and paws. She even checks her tail.

"Meow," says Butter.

Sajés gets Butter's favorite ball and rolls it to her.

Butter does not want to play.

“What’s wrong, Butter?” Chloé asks again.

“Meow,” says Butter.

“If I were a cat, what would I want?” wonders Chloé. “Sajés, let’s make a cat checklist. If we were cats, what would we want?”

“We would want a nice bed,” says Chloé.
They look at Butter’s bed.
“Check,” says Sajés.

"We would want a flea collar," says Chloé.
They look at Butter's flea collar.
"Check," says Sajés.

“We would want fun toys,” says Chloé.
They look at Butter’s toys.
“Check,” says Sajés.

"And we would want good cat food to eat," says Chloé.

They look at Butter's food dish.

"Check," says Sajés.

"Oh, no!" cries Chloé.

"Oh, no!" cries Dad.

“Dad, I know what’s wrong with Butter!” says Chloé.

Butter’s dish is filled with Sajés’s favorite sugary cereal. Her water dish has a juice box in it.

“MEOW!” says Butter.

Chloé cleans out Butter's dishes. Then she fills them with cat food and water.

Butter purrs and starts eating.

Jamie Hector & Alaine Roberson

CHLOÉ WONDERS

Teaching Guide

Written by Pari Deshpande Cohen
Edited by Maria L. Chang, Pari Deshpande Cohen, and Lynne M. Wilson
Illustrations by Rachel Moss
Design by Cynthia Ng

Scholastic Inc., 557 Broadway, New York, NY 10012
Item # 751365

First printing, January 2023.
Printed in Jiaxing, China.
PO#5086171
1 2 3 4 5 6 7 8 9 10 68 31 30 29 28 27 26 25 24 23

SCHOLASTIC

Dear Educator,

Meet Chloé—a smart and curious 7-year-old with a lot of heart. Based on the real-life daughter of author and actor Jamie Hector, Chloé loves to learn new things—and that means asking a lot of questions! Nurturing children's curiosity, as Chloe's family does, is a key component in building self-motivated learners who achieve high academic performance and increased personal well-being.[1] In these books, Chloé asks tons of questions, solves problems, and grows in knowledge and self-understanding.

All children face difficult times, and the ability to cope with challenges is one of the most important skills you can help children cultivate. This teaching guide, written in partnership with the Yale Child Study Center, supports you in this work. Use the Chloé books in conjunction with Yale's resilience framework and the five core competencies from the Collaborative for Academic, Social, and Emotional Learning (CASEL) to help develop children's resilience and social and emotional learning (SEL). The resilience framework guides children to build identity, form relationships, set goals, take action, and think optimistically. SEL helps children develop a healthy understanding of themselves, their emotions, and their relationship to the world around them.[2]

Stories are a powerful tool for helping children build resilience. By seeing a character face a problem, a child can feel less alone. By exploring what a character feels, a child learns to think from other points of view. And by sharing books with others, a child builds community. All of these skills can help your students cope with challenges. The chart on page 3 provides connections between each Chloé book and the Resilience and SEL frameworks. Using the Chloé Wonders set, you will be able to engage in rich discussions, explorations, and class activities that support your students' SEL growth.

In addition, this guide will also help children develop key reading skills at guided reading levels I, J, and K, including:

- building comprehension
- understanding character development and other story elements
- making connections (text to self, text to text, and text to world)

To support comprehension skills and SEL growth, we've included two reproducible pages to go with each book: one focusing on a key reading skill and the other on a specific SEL core competency.

By building resilience, gaining SEL competency, and exploring new literature at the right reading level, children will become adept readers with the skills to be healthy, responsible, and socially aware citizens.

The Editors

[1] https://pubmed.ncbi.nlm.nih.gov/26168378/
[2] Collaborative for Academic, Social, and Emotional Learning. https://casel.org/

Using the Books to Teach Social-Emotional Learning

Each book in this set is designed to build social emotional skills and resilience. Use the connections between the books and the skills below to help your students grow.

Title	SEL Competency	Resilience Framework
Chloé's New Hairdo	**Self-Awareness:** understand one's emotions, thoughts, and values	build pride in self, reframe circumstances form identity
Test Stress	**Self-Management:** manage one's emotions, thoughts, and behaviors	solve problems, reach goals, imagine the future, think optimistically
Sajés's Birthday Feast	**Social Awareness:** understand others' perspectives; build empathy and a sense of belonging	form strong connections, reframe circumstances
Chloé to the Rescue	**Relationship Skills:** establish and maintain healthy relationships	take action, form strong connections
Why Is Butter Sad?	**Responsible Decision-Making:** make constructive choices about behavior and social interactions	solve problems, form strong connections

Connections to the Standards

The lessons in this set support the College and Career Readiness Anchor Standards. These standards, which serve as the basis of many state standards, were developed to establish rigorous educational expectations with the goal of providing students nationwide with a quality education. The chart below details how the lessons align with specific reading standards for literary texts for students in grades 1–2.

LITERARY SKILLS

Key Ideas and Details:

- Ask and answer such questions as *who, what, where, when, why,* and *how* to demonstrate understanding of key details in a text.
- Recount stories and determine their central message, lesson, or moral.
- Describe how characters in a story respond to major events and challenges.

Craft and Structure:

- Identify words and phrases in stories that suggest feelings.
- Describe the overall structure of a story, including describing how the beginning introduces the story and the ending concludes the action.
- Acknowledge differences in the points of view of characters, including by speaking in a different voice for each character when reading dialogue aloud.

Integration of Knowledge and Ideas:

- Use information gained from the illustrations and words in a print or digital text to demonstrate understanding of its characters, setting, or plot.

FOUNDATIONAL SKILLS

Fluency:

- Read with sufficient accuracy and fluency to support comprehension.
- Read grade-level text with purpose and understanding.
- Use context to confirm or self-correct word recognition and understanding, rereading as necessary.

Tips for Using Each Book

Chloé's New Hairdo

Before Reading

Begin by asking children what they think about the title and cover. Ask: *Are hairstyles important to you? Why or why not?* Page through the book together. Think aloud: *I see here (page 5) that Chloé looks sad. I wonder why. Thinking about the title, maybe it has something to do with her hair.*

During Reading

As you read aloud, pause to share your thinking and to ask questions. For example:

- Think aloud on page 6: *I wonder why Chloé thinks her hair "isn't right."*
- Think aloud on page 10: *Chloé looks happier. I think Malika is helping her feel better.*
- Think aloud on page 12: *Wow! That's a lot of different hairstyles! I wonder which one Chloé will pick. This page makes me want to learn more about the different styles people can choose from.*
- Think aloud on page 16: *I'm so happy Chloé discovered that her hair is just right for her and that she loves it! That makes me think of...*

After Reading

Lead discussion about the book. Consider the prompts below to help you facilitate.

- *Have you ever wished you could change something about yourself? What are some things you've done to make yourself feel better about it?* (Make sure not to call on children who don't feel comfortable talking. Share some of your own experiences.)
- *Is Chloé able to share her feelings in a way that helps her solve her problem? How?*
- *Do other people in the story support Chloé? Who helps, and how?*

Test Stress

Before Reading

Ask children to share their thoughts about the cover and title of the book. Ask/define: *What is stress? Have you ever felt stressed? Why? How do you feel when you have a test coming up?* Pointing to Chloé, say: *Chloé looks so sad. I wonder why.*

During Reading

As you read aloud, stop to share your thinking and to ask questions. For example:

- Think aloud on page 3: *I can think of times I thought everyone was better than me at something. It makes me sad to see Chloé feeling this way.*
- Ask on page 4: *Ms. Baker tells Chloé that people fail sometimes. Do you think it's ok to fail? Why or why not? How can failing help you learn?*
- Ask on page 16: *How do you think Chloé will do on this test? Why do you think so?*

After Reading

Invite the class to discuss the book together. Here are some prompts to try.

- *What does Chloé learn to do differently to handle her stress? Do you think it will work?*

- *Sometimes it takes courage to try something new. Does Chloé have courage? What does she learn?*
- *What did you learn about handling stress from reading this book?*

Consider sharing some stress-relief techniques, such as simple breathing exercises, with the class.

Sajés's Birthday Feast

Before Reading

Begin by taking a picture walk through the book. Ask: *What do you notice about the cover?* As you flip through the pages, say: *It looks like there are several words that are not English words. Let's keep an eye out for ways to figure out what each one means.*

During Reading

As you read aloud, pause to share your thinking and to ask questions. For example:

- Think aloud on page 3: *It looks like Grandma Hector speaks another language in addition to English. This makes me think of…*
- Ask on page 5: *How do you think Grandma Hector would feel if she heard Chloé laugh at her? How would you feel if you were her?*
- Ask on page 16: *What does Chloé learn by the end of the book?*

After Reading

Lead discussion about the book. Consider the prompts below to help you facilitate.

- *How does Chloé grow through the course of the book? Does she learn empathy?*
- *Is she able to understand the differences among different groups of people? Does she eventually see differences as a positive thing? How can we tell?*

You may want to show children the different characters' countries of origin as you explore the different cultures and languages shown in this book. Children may also like to share about their own heritages.

Chloé to the Rescue!

Before Reading

Look at the cover and through the pages of the book together. Think aloud: *The title and picture make me think of Chloé as a superhero. I wonder who she's rescuing?* As you flip through the pages, say: *It looks like Sajés is in this book a lot. I wonder if he is the one Chloé rescues.* Ask children: *What is a problem you have needed help with recently? How did you find help?*

During Reading

Pause periodically as you read to ask questions and share your thoughts. For example:

- Think aloud on page 4: *Chloé is asked to help take care of her brother. That's a big job! That reminds me of my family because…*

- Ask on page 4: *Do you have to help out at home? How?*
- Ask on page 5: *How do you think Chloé will solve this problem? What would you do?*
- Think aloud throughout the book: *Chloé is trying hard to solve Sajés's problem and she doesn't give up when she tries something that doesn't work. Do you think she's a good problem solver? Why?*

After Reading

Lead discussion about the book. Consider the prompts below to help you facilitate.

- *Chloé tries a lot of different ways to solve the problem. What do you learn about her character?*
- *Is Chloé able to communicate effectively? Is Sajés?*
- *How does Chloé show leadership? How does she show perseverance?*
- *One relationship skill is offering help and support. How does Chloé do this?*

To build sequencing skills, ask children to retell the series of steps Chloé takes to free Sajés.

Why Is Butter Sad?

Before Reading

Introduce the book by looking at the title and taking a picture walk through the pages. Think aloud: *I wonder who Butter is and why he or she is sad?* As you page through the book, say: *Sajés is in this book a lot. I wonder if Sajés will help Chloé figure out what is wrong with Butter?*

During Reading

As you read aloud, pause to share your thinking and to ask questions. For example:

- Think aloud on page 2: *Why do you think the cat is named Butter?*
- Ask on page 3: *Are you responsible for helping around your house? How?*
- Ask on page 5: *What do you predict is wrong with Butter? How do you think Chloé will find out?*
- Ask on page 14: *What do you think Chloé and Dad see here? They look upset, but Sajés doesn't. Why do you think Sajés isn't upset?*
- Ask on page 15: *Why is Butter unhappy here?*

After Reading

Discuss the book with children. Use the following prompts to help guide the discussion.

- *Why is curiosity important in this book? How does it help Chloé figure out why Butter is sad?*
- *Sajés chooses the food to give Butter. Why is his choice of food not a responsible choice?*
- *What were the effects of Sajés's decision (on all the characters, including Butter)?*

Name: ______________________________

Chloé's New Hairdo

Chloé's feelings change from the beginning to the end of the book. Fill in the chart below. Then answer the question at the bottom of the page.

Beginning of Book	End of Book
Chloé feels ______________________	Chloé feels ______________________
I know this because ______________________ ______________________ ______________________ ______________________	I know this because ______________________ ______________________ ______________________ ______________________

Why did Chloe's feelings change from the beginning to the end of the book?

____

____

____

Name: ______________________________

Chloé's New Hairdo

In the beginning of the book, Chloé feels her hair is not right. By the end of the book, she learns that her hair is unique and is just right for her. What is something that makes you unique or special? Draw and write about it below.

____

____

____

____

____

Name: ______________________________

Test Stress

By the end of the story, Chloé has gained new skills to help her when she feels stressed. How do you think she will do on her next test? How will she feel? Make a prediction in words and in a picture below.

____

____

____

____

Name: ____

Test Stress

Chloé finds that taking deep breaths helps her feel less stressed. When you're feeling worried, sad, or stressed, what are three things you can do to help you feel better?

One thing I can do is ______________________________

____

____

____

Another thing that helps me feel better is

____

____

____

I can also try ______________________________

____

____

____

Name: ______________________________

Sajés's Birthday Feast

Chloé learns a lot from asking questions. What lesson does she learn by the end? Include three details from the story that support your answer.

The lesson Chloé learns is ______________________________

____

____

I know this because

1 ______________________________

____

2 ______________________________

____

3 ______________________________

____

____

Name: ______________________________

Sajés's Birthday Feast

Sajés has friends from many different homelands. Think about a friend of yours who has had different experiences than you have. Then answer the questions below.

What is your friend's name? ______________________

What can you learn from your friend? ______________________

____

____

What can your friend learn from you? ______________________

____

____

Why is it important to have friends who are different from you?

____

____

____

Name: ______________________________

Chloé to the Rescue!

All great stories have a problem and solution. In this story, Chloé helps Sajés solve a problem. Fill in the chart below to show the ways Chloé tries to solve the problem. Then answer the question at the bottom of the page.

What is the problem in the story? ______________________________

____

Chloé tries to solve the problem by:	Does it work? Why or why not?

After reading the story, what is one word you would use to describe Chloé? ______________________________

Why? ______________________________

____

Name: ______________________________

Chloé to the Rescue!

Chloé doesn't just learn how to free Sajés's foot in the book—she also learns to take responsibility and to be a good sister. How does working together help Sajés and Chloé's relationship?

____

____

____

Tell about a time when you helped someone, or when someone helped you. ______________________________

____

____

How did that make you feel? ______________

____

____

____

____

Name: ______________________________

Why Is Butter Sad?

Great writers don't give away all the details—they let readers figure some things out on their own! When we make guesses based on what we observe, we are making *inferences*. Answer the questions below to make inferences about the story.

1. On page 4, Butter is lying down with a paw over her face. What can you infer about how Butter feels?

____

____

2. Dad doesn't want to take Butter to the veterinarian right away. Why not?

____

3. Sajés gives Butter his own favorite foods. What can you infer about Sajés and what he knows about cats?

____

4. What do you think Sajés will give Butter for her meal next time?

____

Name: ______________________________

Why Is Butter Sad?

Sajés chose to feed Butter his favorite foods, but that wasn't the right choice for Butter. Making smart decisions means thinking about all the choices and choosing the best one. Read each sentence below, then think of at least two choices you could make. Tell which is the better choice and why.

Story	Two choices I could make	Which is the better choice? Why?
There is only one cookie left. You and your friend both want it.	• ____________ • ____________	
You are playing ball in the house and break a picture frame.	• ____________ • ____________	
You see a boy trip and fall. Your friend laughs.	• ____________ • ____________	